HOLDING ON

For my lolas Josefina and Benita, and for my grand-aunties Aurora, Presentacion, Cleofas, and Diana, whose love and care have inspired and allowed me to write this story
—S. N. L.

For Mrs. Ro: we'll remember for you
—I. R.

ATHENEUM BOOKS FOR YOUNG READERS
An imprint of Simon & Schuster Children's Publishing Division
1230 Avenue of the Americas, New York, New York 10020
Text © 2022 by Sophia N. Lee
Illustration © 2022 by Isabel Roxas
Book design by Greg Stadnyk © 2022 by Simon & Schuster, Inc.

For information about special discounts for bulk purchases, please contact Simon & Schuster Special Sales at 1-866-506-1949 or business@simonandschuster.com.
The Simon & Schuster Speakers Bureau can bring authors to your live event. For more information or to book an event, contact the Simon & Schuster Speakers Bureau at 1-866-248-3049 or visit our website at www.simonspeakers.com.
The text for this book was set in Neucha.
The illustrations for this book were rendered in mixed media.
Manufactured in China
0422 SCP
First Edition
2 4 6 8 10 9 7 5 3 1
Library of Congress Cataloging-in-Publication Data
Names: Lee, Sophia N., author. | Roxas, Isabel, illustrator.
Title: Holding on / by Sophia N. Lee ; illustrated by Isabel Roxas.
Description: First edition. | New York : Atheneum Books for Young Readers, [2022] | Audience: Ages 4–8. | Audience: Grades K–1. | Summary: A young girl spends song-filled summers with her music-loving grandmother in the Philippines, but when her beloved lola starts slipping into silence and stillness, the girl helps her grandmother hold on with music and the joyful memories the songs bring.
Identifiers: LCCN 2021019366 | ISBN 9781534494459 (hardcover) | ISBN 9781534494466 (ebook)
Subjects: CYAC: Memory—Fiction. | Music—Fiction. | Grandmothers—Fiction. | Old age—Fiction. | LCGFT: Picture books.
Classification: LCC PZ7.1.L429 Ho 2022 | DDC [E]—dc23
LC record available at https://lccn.loc.gov/2021019366

HOLDING ON

SOPHIA N. LEE

Illustrated by
ISABEL ROXAS

Atheneum Books for Young Readers
New York   London   Toronto   Sydney   New Delhi

There is always
singing in Lola's house.

My summers there are filled with so much music.

Frank Sinatra and Sammy Davis Jr. in the morning.

Ella Fitzgerald and Dean Martin in the afternoon.

And in the evening, all the Tagalog love songs I can think of. We listen to Nora Aunor and Basil Valdez sing with so much feeling. They were Lolo's favorites, Lola tells me.

Lola sings and hums and belts along,
fingers dancing, hips swaying.

"If you want to hold on, you gotta
sing your songs," she tells me.

"What do you hold on to, Lola?" I ask.

"You, my little darling," she whispers,
sweeping me up into a hug.

In the winters
when I am away
from Lola, and I'm missing
her hugs the most,
I think of the ways
she holds on.

She holds on to my baby bottle, even though I've grown too big for it.

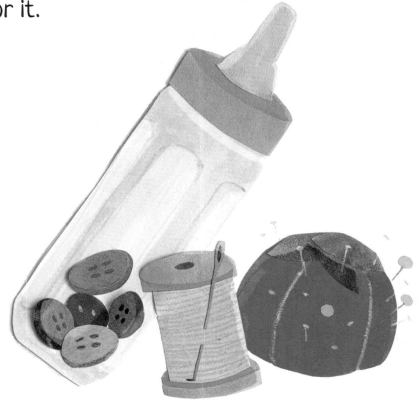

She holds on to my favorite princess pajamas, now too small, by sewing the fabric into a beautiful quilt for colder nights.

She holds on to my favorite childhood dish by making me rice with adobo and mashing ripe bananas to make each bite just a little bit sweeter.

She holds on to the old pictures I drew and hangs them on her walls, next to her favorite pictures of Lolo and of our family.

In my summers with her,
I learn how to hold on too.

I hold the pot still when she stirs the
sinigang and drops the vegetables—
plop, plop—into the broth.

I hold my breath when we listen every night
for Lola's lotto numbers to be drawn.

We close our eyes and imagine all
the things we would do if we won.

I hold her belly when we dance and
sing along to Lolo's favorite songs, hold
her hand even tighter when her voice
breaks, because she's remembering him.

It's important to remember, Lola tells me. So I listen to her stories and remember with her.

We remember the story of when she and Lolo met, how he asked her to dance on the street because he could hear a love song in the distance . . .

and the dress she wore on the day they got married and how smart Lolo looked in his barong Tagalog. We remember how the wedding music made them feel like they were dancing on clouds.

We remember the day I was born, how my loud cries pleased Lola, because it meant I had good, strong lungs.

And we remember how Lola and Mama would sing me to sleep on nights when I woke up fussy.

I learned how to sing because of Lola.
I learned Lola's favorite songs, and then my own.

And her house would be filled with the sound of our memories.

There are days when Lola doesn't remember.

When Lola is quiet. And still.

So I start to sing.

Frank Sinatra and Sammy Davis Jr. in the morning.

Ella Fitzgerald and Dean Martin in the afternoon.

And all throughout the evening, Lolo's favorite Tagalog love songs.

It is my way of being with Lola, of letting her know that it's okay if she doesn't remember sometimes.

I'll remember for her.

I'll hold on to all that she has taught me,
and carry it with me in my heart
and in our songs.

Lola hears the music and smiles.

She stands up and begins to sway.

Fingers dancing, hips grooving.
"If you want to hold on,
you gotta sing your songs," I say.

We sing and hum and belt along.

My summers are always filled with song.